CHILDREN'S THRIFT CLASSICS

Ivanhoe

SIR WALTER SCOTT

Adapted by Bob Blaisdell
Illustrated by John Green

DOVER PUBLICATIONS, INC.
Mineola, New York

DOVER CHILDREN'S THRIFT CLASSICS
EDITOR OF THIS VOLUME: SUSAN L. RATTINER

Copyright

Copyright © 1999 by Dover Publications, Inc.
All rights reserved under Pan American and International Copyright Conventions.

Published in Canada by General Publishing Company, Ltd., 30 Lesmill Road, Don Mills, Toronto, Ontario.
Published in the United Kingdom by Constable and Company, Ltd., 3 The Lanchesters, 162–164 Fulham Palace Road, London W6 9ER.

Bibliographical Note

This Dover edition, first published in 1999, is a new abridgment of a standard text of *Ivanhoe*. The illustrations have been specially prepared for this edition.

Library of Congress Cataloging-in-Publication Data

Scott, Walter, Sir, 1771–1832.
    Ivanhoe / Sir Walter Scott ; adapted by Bob Blaisdell ; illustrated by John Green.
        p.   cm. — (Dover children's thrift classics)
    "This Dover edition . . . is a new abridgment of a standard text of Ivanhoe. The illustrations have been specially prepared for this edition"— T.p. verso.
    Summary: An abridgment of the novel chronicling the adventures of the Saxon knight Ivanhoe in 1194, the year of Richard the Lion-Hearted's return from the Third Crusade.
    ISBN 0-486-40143-X (pbk.)
    1. Great Britain—History—Richard I, 1189–1199—Juvenile fiction. [1. Great Britain—History—Richard I, 1189–1199—Fiction. 2. Knights and knighthood—Fiction.] I. Blaisdell, Robert. II. Green, John, ill. III. Title. IV. Series.
PZ7.S43Iv   1999
[Fic]—dc21   97–44614
                                                    CIP
                                                   AC

Manufactured in the United States of America
Dover Publications, Inc., 31 East 2nd Street, Mineola, N.Y. 11501

Contents

A herald sounds the trumpet, the signal to begin the tournament.

1. The Disinherited Knight

IT WAS nearly eight hundred years ago that King Richard of England was imprisoned in distant Austria by his very own brother, Prince John, and his enemies King Philip of France and the cruel Duke of Austria. John meant to become king of England himself, and to do so he befriended the Norman noblemen who lorded over most of the land. He allowed them to make miserable the poor, hard-working Saxon people whose ancestors had once ruled England.

But not all bent to the hard rule of the French-speaking Normans. There were many, for example Robin Hood and his Merry Men, who banded together and claimed the forests for themselves. Others continued to live in their ancestral dwellings, for instance Cedric and his ward, the young and beautiful Rowena. Cedric and Rowena were descended from the royal line of Saxons, and kept alive the hope that their people's glory days that preceded the last hundred years would return.

In spite of the long and lingering Saxon resentment of the Normans, all the people of England enjoyed the chivalric tournaments that the Normans had brought to this island kingdom. The tournaments featured jousting contests between armored knights, archery competitions, music, and other entertainment. At the time of our story, just such a tournament was taking place in a large meadow near the town of Ashby in the region of Leicester.

To the south of the field, or lists, was the forest, while off to the west the meadow was fringed by oak trees. By midmorning there were several thousand spectators gathered around the field. At two ends were gates, each manned by heralds to announce, with a team of six trumpeters, the jousting competitors.

Along one side were five large tents with red and black banners streaming in the sunny day's light breeze. There were colorfully decorated stands alongside the field for the noblemen and women, who were costumed as elegantly as the commoners were raggedly. In front of the stands, just in back of the lists' boundary lines, was a narrow space for those with some money yet without noble status. Among them were two we shall see more of in the course of our story, the beautiful and wise Rebecca and her father, Isaac. To Isaac it was that Prince John and other nobles came for loans when they meant to hire soldiers to stamp out the Saxon rebels. Though they did not accept him in their social world because of his being Jewish, they depended on Isaac's ability to raise money for them.

Hundreds of peasants who could not crowd alongside the jousting field had found space upon low surrounding banks; others perched themselves on the branches of trees which surrounded the meadow; even the steeple of a country church, at some distance, was crowded with spectators. All wanted to see the upcoming jousts, as the red and black outfitted Knights of the Templars, famous for their fighting skill in the distant Crusades, were to compete against any who were brave or foolish enough to challenge them.

On the east side of the field was a set of stands, in the very center of which was a platform raised higher than the others; it was richly decorated, and had a large, open tent over a throne. As of yet, only servants appeared on this platform; they were awaiting the arrival of Prince John and his close advisers. On the other side of the narrow field, exactly opposite the royal throne, was another set of stands, decorated with tapestries and carpets, with a seat of honor there designated for the "Queen of Love and Beauty." Who that queen was to be, everyone wondered but no one knew.

Suddenly there was a hubbub as Prince John, upon his spirited and fancifully decorated horse, entered through the gate at the north end of the field, followed and accompanied by dozens of noblemen and church leaders. He was splendidly dressed in red and gold; on his leather-gloved hand was perched a watchful falcon, its beautiful eyes as haughty as the prince's own. On Prince John's head was a fur bonnet, dotted with a circle of precious stones, from which his long curled hair flowed onto his

Prince John entered through the gate
upon his fancifully decorated horse.

shoulders. He gazed about him at the handsome men and beautiful women in the stands and along the field, not seeming to see anyone in particular until he noticed Rebecca. She was as gorgeous as any woman in England, but because she was Jewish she wore Eastern dress—a vested gown of purple silk, with gold clasps, and upon her head a turban of yellow silk adorned with an ostrich feather. Her eyes flashed like jewels and her teeth were as white as pearls. Her black tresses fell in long spiraling curls over her shoulders.

"What is she, Isaac?" called out Prince John. "Is she your wife or daughter?"

"My daughter Rebecca, so please your grace," answered Isaac.

Gazing about him along the field,
Prince John suddenly noticed Rebecca.

"She should be seated above, in the stands with the nobles! We have forgotten," Prince John said, turning to his closest adviser, "to name the Queen of Love and Beauty."

"Nay, nay," said De Bracy, the nobleman who rode alongside the prince, "let the fair queen's throne remain unoccupied, until the conquerer shall be named, and then let *him* choose the lady by whom it shall be filled."

Prince John thought this a wise decision, and he agreed to it. He smiled once more upon Rebecca, who did not, in her turn, smile back. John and the others now dismounted from their horses and marched up into their places in the stands. John sat down on the throne, took a deep breath, and nodded to one of his servants. That servant gave the signal to the senior, clear-voiced herald to come forward and announce, for all to hear, the rules of the day's tournament.

"Rule number one!" called the herald. "The five heroic, crusading knights from the temple are to accept any other knight's offer of combat.

"Rule number two! A knight may choose one particular Templar with whom to do battle. He does so by touching with his lance the shield of the other. If he does so with the handle of the lance, this fight shall take place with the so-called 'arms of courtesy.' The lances, therefore, will be tipped with a rounded board, so that less danger will result from the impact. However, if the knight chooses a Templar and touches his shield with the pointed end of the lance, the knights must fight as in actual battle, with sharp weapons.

"Number three! When the five Templar Knights have fulfilled their quest of breaking five lances each of their opponents, Prince John shall declare the winner of today, the first of two days in this tournament. He shall receive a warhorse as his prize . . . and, in addition, an unexpected prize of naming the tournament's Queen of Love and Beauty!

"Tomorrow, on the tournament's second day, there shall be a general tournament, in which all the knights present may take part. They will divide into two bands of equal numbers to fight it out manfully, until the signal is given by Prince John to cease the combat. Today's Queen of Love and Beauty is then to crown the knight whom the prince calls the best fighter of the second day."

*A crowd of armored knights gathered in the field,
eager to fight the fierce Normans.*

Before the rules were completely announced, there was a clamoring, clanking crowd of armored knights gathering at the far end of the field. These warriors, younger or less experienced than the Templars, were eager to try their skill against the fierce Normans. The nobles, from their comfortable places in the stands, saw the distant unnamed knights as a sea of waving feathers attached to polished, glistening helmets. The knights' tall lances had small pennants attached to them, which, like the feathers atop the helmets, fluttered in the breeze.

In a few moments, the gate at the far end was opened, and five knights came riding slowly into the lists. There was one knight in front, the designated leader, with the other four in two pairs behind. Every spectator leaned forward to watch them as they neared the Templars' pavilions. In front of each pavilion there hung the knight's shield. The Knights of the Temple were standing beside their tents as they awaited the first challenge of the day. Each of the five daring knights tapped the Templars' shields with the handle-end of their lances, thus making it a fight with rounded tips.

The Templars smiled among themselves at the sport before them, and the five opposing knights retreated to the far side of the field, where they arranged themselves in a line. The Norman Templars pulled their helmets on, collected their shields and mounted their horses. Their leader was the hard-hearted Brian de Bois-Guilbert, the bravest of them all and the keenest fighter. The Templars lined themselves up exactly opposite the knights who had challenged them.

All was ready. Prince John gave a royal nod, and the heralds signalled the trumpeters, who blew a loud note. At that sound, the knights started their horses at full gallop. In two moments there was a furious crash of wood upon metal, as the Templars' lances smashed three of their opponents to the ground. Bois-Guilbert, Sir Philip Malvoisin and Reginald Front-de-Boeuf had fully conquered their challengers. One of the unknown knights disgracefully swerved from the line of Hugh de Grantmesnil's lance, while the last, maintaining his team's honor, kept his seat, in spite of splintering his lance against the Knight of St. John's shield.

The crowd shouted with admiration; the heralds called out the names of the victors; the trumpeters blew some lofty notes. Prince John chuckled, and the nobles remarked to each other upon the famous Templars, valiant warriors who had lustily carried the name of Christianity to the infidels of the East.

After the first round, a second, third, and then fourth party of unknown knights came out to challenge the Templars. With the completion of each new contest, the trumpets announced that the formidable victors of the first round had won again.

Not one of the Templars ever found himself knocked from his seat, and in every round Brian de Bois-Guilbert unseated his opponent. After the fourth round there was a very long pause in the action; it did not appear that anyone wanted to take on the stalwart Normans. Prince John began to talk to his servants about getting the victory banquet ready.

"It seems," he said to De Bracy, "that Bois-Guilbert will win the warhorse today. I wonder if he will award the Queen of Beauty to Rebecca, as I would?"

Meanwhile, the noblemen and women heaved a sigh; the jousting seemed at an end. But then, suddenly, from the far end of the field came the blare of a single trumpet. All eyes turned to see the new knight which this sound announced, and no sooner was the gate opened than upon a black horse he entered the lists. It was not easy to tell very much about a knight clad in armor, but he did not seem to be a large man. His armor was well-made—steel, with golden trim. Upon his shield was a design of gold: a young oak tree pulled up by the roots, with the word "Disinherited" engraved beneath it. As he rode across the grass he gracefully waved to Prince John and the ladies upon the neighboring stands.

He now came to the Templars' pavilions. To the surprise of all, he stopped in front of Brian de Bois-Guilbert and, using the sharp and dangerous end of the lance, touched the knight's shield.

Bois-Guilbert could hardly believe such a challenge to

Using the sharp end of the lance,
he touched the shield of Brian de Bois-Guilbert.

himself. "You peril your life so recklessly?" asked the Knight of the Templars.

"My life is secure compared to yours," answered the Disinherited Knight.

"Bah! Take your place on the field," said Bois-Guilbert, "and have a last look at the sun; because tonight you shall sleep forever after in heaven."

The Disinherited Knight replied, "I advise *you* to fetch a fresh horse and a new lance, for by my honor you will need both." He reined his horse backward and returned to the southern end of the field, where he awaited the Templar.

For a moment, Bois-Guilbert was so angry he wanted to rush immediately after the daring challenger. But on second thought, he did change his hard-worked horse for a fresh, strong one. He asked his squire for a selection of new spears, and after gripping and weighing two or three, found a new one to his liking. Finally, he equipped himself with a new shield, as the other, decorated with the humble picture of two knights of the Temple upon one horse, had a few dents. The design on his new shield showed a raven clutching a skull in its claws, the words beneath this image stating: "BEWARE THE RAVEN!"

He now rode out upon his lively horse, his opponent waiting patiently.

As soon as the trumpets gave the signal, the knights rushed from their spots with the speed of lightning and closed in the center of the field with the shock of a thunderbolt. Their lances exploded into splinters up to the very handles, and it seemed for a moment that both knights would fall off to the ground, for the shock of the impact had made each horse recoil upon its back legs. But the riders recovered control of their steeds and retired to the ends of the field, where they each received a fresh lance from the attendants.

The spectators in the stands rose from their seats, and every onlooker gave a loud shout of excitement. The ladies in the galleries waved scarves, and the commoners waved handkerchiefs. King John refrained from shouting, but he stood nearly on tiptoes, lest a waving scarf block his sight.

The two snorting horses resumed their positions, and the men atop them glared through their visors across the field at each other. They were ready to joust again. The crowd fell silent, almost holding its breath with anticipation.

Prince John waved to the heralds, who signalled the trumpeters to sound the charge. They did so, and the knights upon their horses sprung from their posts. In the

*The knights clashed in the center of the field,
their lances exploding into splinters.*

center of the field they again met with a terrible clamor, but this time one of them fell.

The Templar had aimed his lance at the very center of the Disinherited Knight's shield, and he had struck it so forcefully that the lance cracked into shivers, almost sending the other knight tumbling. On the other hand, the Disinherited Knight had at the last moment changed the aim of his lance from his opponent's shield to the helmet. What a difficult mark to hit, but hit it the Disinherited Knight did, and with a startling impact. The lance gripped the Norman knight's visor and plunged him, and his horse, to the ground, tearing a swath in the grassy field. The famous warrior was embarrassed and enraged; in an instant, he rose from the turf.

The crowd roared with pleasure, cheering at the surprising result.

Bois-Guilbert, angry with them and with this knight, drew his sword. The grass of the field was in his mouth and nose, and he waved the sword at his conqueror, calling, "Taste this!"

"Gladly!" said the Disinherited Knight, leaping from his horse in an instant. He pulled out his sword, but the tournament's marshals, like early-day referees, came riding between them.

"There is no such fighting allowed, knights!" they warned them. "The tournament has rules against this!"

"Then we shall meet again," called the Templar to the Disinherited Knight, "and where there are none to separate us."

"On foot or horseback, with spear, with axe, or with sword, I am ready to encounter you," replied his foe.

The Disinherited Knight returned to his post, where he announced the dedication of his victory "To all true English hearts, and to the overthrow of foreign tyrants." He then told the herald, "I am now ready to face any challengers, one at a time, in any order they please."

One after another, Bois-Guilbert's comrades rode out to

challenge the Disinherited Knight, and one after another, he sent them sprawling to the turf.

All were impressed by the unknown warrior's power, and none had ever seen such a display by a single knight in a single tournament. There was no choice for Prince John but to award the championship of the day to the Disinherited Knight.

"But, please," said one of the marshals to the mysterious, unnamed knight, "we ask that you take your helmet off before you accept the prize from Prince John."

The Disinherited Knight shook his head, saying, "I cannot. I must not allow my face to be seen at this time."

The marshals gave up their request, and led the knight to the royal pavilion. Smilingly, Prince John turned to his friends and advisers, and said, "What do you think, my lords—who is this gallant knight?"

A whisper arose among them. "It might be the King—it might be Richard the Lion-Hearted himself!"

"Waldemar! De Bracy!" called the suddenly frightened prince to his closest advisers. "Brave knights and gentlemen, remember your promises and stand truly by me."

"Here is no danger," said Waldemar Fitzurse; "have you forgotten how gigantic your brother is? Richard would never fit into that suit of armor. Look at this knight more closely. Your Highness will see that he is shorter than King Richard, and much less broad across the shoulders. This is a younger, smaller man, to be sure. The very horse he rides could not have supported Richard's weight."

Even as Fitzurse spoke, the marshals had reached the pavilion with the champion. They waited at the foot of the stairs leading to the throne.

Prince John, even with the reassurance of his friend, was nervous about this knight. Maybe, somehow, it was indeed his own brother, the rightful king and wrongfully treated ruler.

"Ahem," he said, clearing his throat. "Brave knight— brave, nameless knight, you who have lost your inheri-

tance somewhere, somehow—you have proved yourself
skillful and valiant, and I award you the warhorse, as described earlier by my herald." There was no immediate response, and again Prince John was terrified that the voice
from within that helmet would be his brother's.

The knight only made a low bow, as if thanking the
prince for his words.

"Very well, silent knight," said Prince John, carefully
peering down upon the masked warrior, "you must now, in
addition to receiving your first prize, name the woman
who is to be the tournament's Queen of Love and
Beauty.—Now hold out your lance."

The Disinherited Knight obeyed, and the prince placed
upon the lance's point a green satin crown, trimmed with
brilliant gold.

*With a crown upon his lance, the Disinherited Knight rode slowly,
seeking out the Queen of Love and Beauty.*

"Award that crown to the lady of your choice," said Prince John.

Again the knight bowed, and then he backed his horse away, and rode slowly to and fro along the foot of the stands, seeking out the most lovely of the many beautiful faces.

Finally he came to a stop in front of the Saxon named Rowena. She was sitting in the first row of the stands, beside her guardian, Cedric the Saxon, the aging warrior who had renounced his own son, Ivanhoe, for serving the Norman king, Richard, on his Crusades to the Holy Land. Once, he had hoped for Rowena to wed his son, but disobedience on Ivanhoe's part had changed Cedric's mind. Cedric now looked for her to marry Athelstane, a dull, slow-witted man descended from the last of the Saxon monarchs of England.

Many seconds passed as the Disinherited Knight seemed to study the fair face of Rowena, who blushingly averted her gaze from the warrior's.

Then, as gradually and gracefully as could be, the knight sank the point of his lance at her feet, the crown sliding off into her possession. At that very moment the trumpets sounded, and the heralds proclaimed her the Queen of Love and Beauty.

There followed repeated shouts of "Long live Lady Rowena, the Queen of Love and of Beauty!"

The Disinherited Knight now turned away, and rode off across the field, leading his new, prize warhorse through the far gate. He rode with many spectators trailing after him along the edge of the wood until he came to a large tent, where he dismounted and handed over the reins of both horses to a strange, brown-hooded man who was awaiting him. In spite of the many offers from onlookers to come within and help him or bring him food, the knight waved their curiosity away, and disappeared within the tent.

Everyone desired to know who the knight was who had refused to lift his visor or to name his name.

2. Wilfred of Ivanhoe

THE NEXT morning, before the sun was even much above the horizon, eager spectators began appearing on the meadow. They looked forward to further jousting, and secured for themselves the best places to watch the contest.

The marshals then appeared on the field to begin, with the heralds, the job of collecting the names of the knights who wanted to joust in the day's battle. According to the rules of the tournament, the Disinherited Knight was to be the leader of one side, while Brian de Bois-Guilbert was to lead the other.

By ten o'clock, the whole plain was crowded with horsemen, horsewomen, and foot-passengers hurrying to the tournament; and shortly after, a grand flourish of trumpets announced Prince John and his following. About the same time Cedric the Saxon arrived with Lady Rowena. She was tall, fair, with clear blue eyes and dark eyebrows. Her hair was full, dark-blond, and arranged elaborately in numerous ringlets, with gems braided within them. She wore a golden chain around her neck and bracelets on her wrists; many admired her long dress of pale green silk, over which hung a robe, which reached to the ground, having very wide sleeves. This robe was crimson, of the finest wool. A silk veil, interwoven with gold, was attached to the upper part of it, which could be either drawn over the face and bosom or draped over the shoulders. Meanwhile, Athelstane, her suitor since Ivanhoe had been renounced by Cedric, wore armor in order to take his place among the day's fighters. He had been jealous of the Disinherited Knight's attentions the previous day to Rowena and wished to take some revenge on the mysterious champion.

As soon as Prince John saw that the queen of the day had arrived, he rode forward to meet her, doffed his hat in welcome, and led her to the seat of honor opposite his own. The senior herald then went forward onto the lists to proclaim the laws of the tournament.

"Hear ye, hear ye, knights of the joust! You may not thrust with your swords, for such is the deadly stroke! You may strike but not thrust! You may use a mace or battle-axe, but you may not use a dagger! If you are knocked off your horse, you may fight any knights from the opposite side who are also on foot. As soon as Prince John throws down his staff the combat must cease!"

When the announcement of these rules was complete, the participants began riding onto the lists from the two gates. They arranged themselves in two lines, opposite each other, with the leader of each team in the center of the first row. The horses were snorting, eager for the fight to begin, when, finally, a marshal called out, "Go to and battle!"

The trumpets sounded as he spoke, and the two front rows of each team rushed upon each other in full gallop and met in the middle of the field with a shock, the sound of which was heard at a mile's distance. The dust raised by so many steeds made it impossible for spectators to see the result of the first conflict. By the time the dust settled, half the knights on each side were off their horses—some lay stretched on the ground as if they would never get up again—and several on both sides had received bloody wounds or suffered broken limbs. Almost all of the knights who had remained upon their horses had broken their lances against their opponents' shields. They now took on each other with swords as they shouted terrible war cries and exchanged blows.

The clangs of the swords against metal and the shouts of the combatants drowned out the sound of the groans of those who fell. The armor of the knights, once so shiny, was now dusty and bloody. Between every pause of the angry crashes of steel the heralds could be heard exclaiming, "Fight on, brave knights! Man dies, but glory lives. Fight on, brave knights, for bright eyes behold your deeds!"

The Disinherited Knight and Bois-Guilbert kept trying to single out each other, but there were so many other knights and so much confusion that they could not get in range to strike. But then, as the fight wore on, the crowd of warriors became thinner as a dozen or more on either side fell to the field. Now the Templar and the Disinherited Knight met each other hand to hand.

But it was not to be a fair fight, as two knights from Brian de Bois-Guilbert's side (one of whom was jealous Athelstane, the Saxon) came rushing over to help attack the Disinherited Knight. Their one goal was to knock the lone hero from his horse and then kill him with their swords.

Nothing could have saved the Disinherited Knight except the remarkable strength of the noble horse which he had won the previous day. As it scampered to and fro, he was able to keep at sword's point his three enemies, rushing now against one, now against another, dealing sweeping, clanging blows.

But although the spectators clapped their hands for his bravery and nimble work, everyone believed that sooner or later his enemies would overpower him. However, there was a surprise in store for all, and it changed the fortune of the day.

Among the two dozen warriors on the Disinherited Knight's team, there was one in black armor, on a black horse. There was no identifying symbol or image on his shield, and up until now he had hardly waved his sword.

*One of the warriors on the Disinherited Knight's team
had no identifying symbol on his shield.*

"What a sluggard that one is," remarked De Bracy, Prince
John's adviser. "He should have sat in the stands with the
rest of us, for all the activity he shows!"

But all at once this knight set spurs to his horse and
came to the Disinherited Knight's assistance like a

thunderbolt, exclaiming, "To the rescue!" It was high time; for, while the Disinherited Knight was fighting the Templar, Front-de-Boeuf had got near to him with an uplifted sword; but before the blow could fall, the Black Knight dealt a stroke on Front-de-Boeuf's helmet, which caused Bois-Guilbert's comrade to tumble to the ground. Upon impact with Front-de-Boeuf's helmet, the Black Knight's sword broke, so the "Sluggard" wrenched a battle-axe from the hand of Athelstane.

The Black Knight immediately swung his arm around and dealt Athelstane such a blow upon the head that the Saxon was sent springing from his saddle. Athelstane fell in a senseless heap upon the field. Having conquered two warriors in a matter of seconds, the Black Knight slowly rode off to the northern end of the field, leaving his leader to cope as he best could, and all alone, with Brian de Bois-Guilbert. The Disinherited Knight charged the Templar, and with a crash of steel upon the Norman's armor, sent Bois-Guilbert rolling off his horse and onto the field. Hearing his enemy curse him, the Disinherited Knight leaped from his horse, waved his sword over the head of Bois-Guilbert, and commanded him to give up.

Prince John jumped up from his throne and cast down his staff, putting an end to the tournament and saving the Norman knight from admitting defeat.

Though the prince was displeased with the results, it was now his duty to name the most valiant knight. He said, "The honor of the day belongs to the Black Knight."

The heralds called for the Black Knight to present himself before the prince. But to the surprise of the spectators and participants, the "Sluggard" who had rescued the Disinherited Knight was nowhere to be found. A few spectators had noticed that he had left the field immediately when the prince threw down the staff, and then had ridden away, into the forest.

"Blow the trumpets!" cried the senior herald. "Perhaps the favored knight is hard of hearing."

But even after the mighty blasts of the deep-breathed trumpeters, there was no response from and no return of the Black Knight. "You must name another champion, Prince John," whispered another of John's advisers.

"Must I? Then it must be, unfortunately, the winner of yesterday's contest, the Disinherited Knight. But someone must make sure he is unmasked today," said the nervous brother of the bold and great King Richard. "I will not address a faceless man again."

"Come along," the marshals told the Disinherited Knight. "For the second day in a row, you are the champion." They led him to the foot of John's throne, where the prince stood up and, nodding to the marshals, said, "Disinherited Knight, we award you the honors of the tournament, and announce to you your right to claim and receive from the hands of the Queen of Love and Beauty the garland of honor which your valor deserves." The knight bowed low, but returned no answer.

On the lower step of Lady Rowena's throne the champion was made to kneel down. Rowena, stepping down from her tournament throne, was about to place the flowered garland which she held in her hands upon the Disinherited Knight's helmet, when the marshals exclaimed, "It must not be this way—his head must be bare!"

When the knight, startled by this command, cried out, "Heavens no!" the marshals paid no attention. They pulled knives from their belts and quickly cut the laces that tied the helmet to his armor. They lifted off the helmet and revealed the handsome, sun-tanned face of a twenty-five-year-old. He looked to be in pain, and his face and hair were streaked with blood.

The moment Rowena saw this face she nearly shrieked; how she recovered her wits, she never knew, but she continued the ceremony by saying, "Sir Knight, Wilfred of Ivanhoe, I award you this garland. Never was there a more worthy hero!"

The knight stooped his head and kissed the hand of the lovely queen, and then, sinking and sinking yet farther forward, collapsed at her feet.

Of course there was instant amazement and confusion. Cedric the Saxon, who had been struck dumb by the sud-

The knight stooped his head and kissed the hand of the lovely queen.

den appearance of his banished (and disinherited) son Ivanhoe, now rushed forward through the spectators. The marshals of the field immediately guessed that the cause of Ivanhoe's swoon was a deep wound, and so undid his armor. There they found that the head of a lance had broken through his breastplace and gashed him through his side.

The name of Ivanhoe was no sooner uttered than it flew from mouth to mouth: "Who? Ivanhoe! Can that mean that King Richard is far behind?" It was not long before the name of Ivanhoe reached the circle of advisers around the prince, who frowned as he heard the news. A moment later a mysterious letter was put into his hands.

John read the few words within it: "Watch out for yourself! Your enemy is free!" The prince turned as pale as death. "It means," he told his supporters Fitzurse and De Bracy, "that the king, my brother Richard, has obtained his freedom."

"It is time, then," said Fitzurse, "to draw up plans to deal with this by readying our attack upon him. We must call a conference of allies in York. A few days later and it will be too late. Your Highness must break short this tournament."

The sound of trumpets soon brought attention to Prince John's announcement, who said he had been suddenly called by public duties and was forced to end the festival.

When Cedric had seen his son fall in a heap on the field, his first impulse was to claim him and bring him into his care, but the words choked in his throat. He could not bring himself to say, in front of the hated Normans, that this was his own Ivanhoe, the disobedient son whom he had sworn never to see again. He ordered, however, Oswald, his servant, to keep an eye upon him; and directed Oswald to bring Ivanhoe to him as soon as the crowd had dispersed. But before Oswald could manage to get close to Ivanhoe, the knight had disappeared.

When Ivanhoe had sunk down, it was Rebecca who told her father to have the gallant young warrior carried from the field to their temporary lodgings near Ashby.

"Holy Abraham!" Isaac exclaimed. "He is a good man,

but to carry him to our house! Damsel, have you thought about the consequences to us?"

"When a Christian is wounded and in misery, he becomes the Jew's brother," replied Rebecca.

"But if he does not recover!" cautioned Isaac. "If he dies in our custody, won't we be held responsible?"

"He will not die, Father. He will not die," said Rebecca calmly, "unless we abandon him."

She had their servants carry Ivanhoe on a stretcher all the way back to Ashby. Once there, Rebecca examined her patient and treated and bound up his wounds. In the Dark Ages, many females knew the arts of doctoring, and the Jews, both male and female, practiced medicine. Beautiful Rebecca had been taught all known medical knowledge by an old and wise Jewess, and her strong mind had continued to learn. Smart and lovely, Rebecca was held in high regard by her tribe.

When Ivanhoe reached Isaac's dwelling, he was still unconscious, for he had lost much blood. Rebecca examined the wound, and cleaned it, and rubbed in a healing ointment. She told her father that if Ivanhoe did not come down with a fever, there was nothing to fear, and that the brave and handsome knight might safely travel to York with them the next day.

It was not until evening was almost over that Ivanhoe came to. He awoke but was unable for some time to remember what had happened at the tournament and how he had come to be here. He found himself in a magnificently furnished room. He thought it odd that there were no chairs, only cushions, to sit on. As he was groggily taking in the details of the room, a curtain was drawn aside, and a beautiful female, dressed in a luxurious Eastern gown, glided through a door. She was followed by a burly male servant.

As Ivanhoe, aching with pain, was about to speak to this woman, she shook her head and placed a finger on her lips. "You must not speak. You must lie still and rest." Her

As Ivanhoe awoke, a beautiful female glided through a door.

servant approached the wounded knight and gently un-
covered the blanket from Ivanhoe's side. Rebecca leaned
close and made sure the bandage was in place and the
wound doing well.

"Kind maiden," groaned Ivanhoe, "noble damsel . . ."

"Do not use the term 'noble' for me, Sir Knight," she
said. "You should know that your nurse is a poor Jewess,
the daughter of Isaac." She told him they needed to return
to York, and that she would nurse him until his health

came back. "The Saxons in this country might take you in," she said, "but no Christian doctor within the four seas of Britain could heal you so well or swiftly as I."

"And how soon will you be able to heal me?"

"Within eight days, if you will be patient and obey my directions," replied Rebecca. "Let me tell you what you cannot have known. Prince John has broken off the tournament, and set forward with all haste towards York, with the nobles, knights and churchmen of his party, after collecting such sums of gold as they could wring from my people. It is said he means to try to take his brother's crown and plant himself on the king's throne."

"Not without a blow struck by me in Richard's defense," said Ivanhoe, raising himself with agony upon the couch. "I will fight for Richard's rights."

"But that you may be able to do so," said Rebecca, touching his shoulder with her hand, "you must now observe my directions and remain quiet. Have faith that your strength shall soon help your people. Take the medicine, so that you may be the more able to bear the journey tomorrow."

Ivanhoe obeyed her, and in the morning his kind doctor found him entirely free of feverish symptoms and fit to undergo the journey. He was placed on a well-covered stretcher, which was hitched up behind a sure-footed quiet horse, and they set out through the forest for York.

3. The Battle of Torquilstone Castle

AT THE SAME time as Rebecca, Isaac, their servants, and Ivanhoe were winding their way through the forest, Cedric, Athelstane (dizzy, but otherwise recovered from the Black Knight's fearsome blow), Rowena, and their servants were journeying through it as well. They were on their way to Cedric's humble Saxon mansion. They were surprised to suddenly hear repeated cries for help; and when they rode up to the site of the uproar, they found a covered stretcher placed upon the ground, beside which sat a young woman, richly dressed in the Jewish fashion, while an old man, whose yellow cap showed him to be Jewish as well, walked up and down in despair. This was of course Isaac, who explained that he had hired a bodyguard of six men at Ashby, together with mules for carrying the stretcher of a sick friend to York. They had come this far in safety; but then the bodyguards heard that a band of Normans was lying in wait in the woods, and they had run off, leaving their employers to fend for themselves.

Rebecca had recognized Cedric and Rowena at once, but she kept Ivanhoe hidden, trusting more in her own medicine than in the rough Saxon treatment of the sick and wounded. She felt that if Cedric saw his son in such a woeful condition, he would surely take charge of him—but to no good end, despite the best intentions. Isaac, for his part, dared not reveal to Cedric that the stretcher bore

27

Ivanhoe, because he feared the Saxon's quick and violent wrath for having kidnapped his son, even though it was clearly to the son's good.

Cedric believed Isaac's story, and ordered the servants to hitch up mules to the well-covered stretcher. At Rowena's request, Cedric agreed to make a detour to a spot at the edge of the forest near York, so that Rebecca, Isaac, and the "sick one" would be safe.

The path through the woods which had once been the width of a road, now narrowed, and there was hardly room for two men to walk side by side. Their small group was in no order to defend themselves, and when they had just crossed a small stream, they were attacked all at once in front, sides, and rear.

They were made prisoners with almost no fight, and only one of Cedric's party was able to escape, a jester named Wamba. He threw himself into the underbrush and scurried from the scene of action.

Yet this jester, as soon as he was safe, hesitated whether he should not turn back and allow himself to be captured. "I have heard men talk of the blessings of freedom," he said aloud to himself, for in some ways he was little more than Cedric's slave, "but I wish any wise man would teach me what use to make of freedom now that I have it."

As he spoke those words, a voice very near him called out, "Wamba!"

"Gurth!" answered Wamba, and Gurth the swineherd, who had been acting as Ivanhoe's servant since the hero's return to England, came forward. Gurth had been closely and secretly following Isaac's caravan, and had been about to help them when Cedric appeared. He hid himself away, so that Cedric would not put two and two together and realize that the young man on the stretcher was his disinherited son. Gurth had faith in Rebecca's powers as a healer, and wanted her to have every opportunity to save Ivanhoe.

Gurth and Wamba were old friends, and they now dis-

A man, dressed in green and carrying a long bow,
suddenly appeared before Gurth and Wamba.

cussed the terrible situation their masters were in, and
wondered how they would be able to save them. But then
a third man, dressed in green, with a long bow and a fine
bugle, suddenly appeared before their eyes. He waved a
sword at them and told them to be quiet. "You don't know
me, but I know who those men are who captured your
friends and masters. They are Templars and Norman nobles, friends of Prince John. We three men alone cannot
try to rescue our comrades; that would be madness, for
their captors are wicked but brave knights. Come, then,
with me, until I gather such a force as may overcome
them."

It was after three hours of walking that Gurth and Wamba, with their guide, who said his name was Locksley, arrived at a small opening in the forest, in the center of which grew an enormous oak tree. Beneath this tree four or five young men lay stretched on the ground, while another, as look-out, walked to and fro in the moonlight shade.

Locksley immediately began ordering them to collect the others and to call the Friar, whom they could hear singing with a companion in the hut nearby. "Two of you take the road quickly towards Torquilstone, the Castle of Front-de-Boeuf. A pack of Norman dogs is driving a band of prisoners there. Watch them closely."

Soon the Friar appeared with, of all people, the Black Knight, whom he introduced as a lost traveler. Locksley, who in disguise had attended the tournament the day before, recognized the Black Knight, and led him a short distance apart from the others. "Don't deny it, Sir Knight—you are the one who came to the rescue of the Disinherited Knight and smashed those Normans at the tournament. In such case, are you our friend as well?"

"I am," replied the Black Knight.

"But are you a good Englishman as well as a good knight?"

"You can speak to no one," replied the knight, "to whom England, and the life of every Englishman, can be dearer than to me."

"Then let me tell you that a band of villains has made itself master of Cedric the Saxon, with his ward Rowena and his friends, and have hauled them to a castle called Torquilstone. I ask of you, as a good knight and a good Englishman, will you help us save them?"

"By my vow as a knight I am bound to help the unfortunate."

Locksley's men, the Black Knight, Gurth, and Wamba set out through the forest to Torquilstone. They were worried about the fate of their friends. They had good cause to worry, though little did they know that Isaac was chained in the dungeon, while beautiful Rebecca was harassed by a new admirer, the Templar Brian de Bois-Guilbert. Meanwhile, De Bracy, one of Prince John's traitorous advisers, was trying to woo Rowena, who, ever since seeing Ivanhoe wounded at her feet the day before, had been unable to think of anyone else's troubles, including those of herself and Cedric. She did not know that in a tower within that very castle, Rebecca, when not harassed by Bois-Guilbert, was nursing Ivanhoe.

Down below, in the forest surrounding the castle, Locksley and the Black Knight came up with a plan for entering the well-defended and imposing castle: the jester would dress himself up as a poor hermit, ask the Normans to let him in for charity's sake, and then find out the whereabouts of the captives and the plans of the enemy.

While his companions watched from the woods, Wamba the jester trudged forward with his head bowed, a priest's cowl covering his eyes, until he was stopped at the castle gate.

"Who are you and what do you want here?" asked the guard.

"Peace to you," said the jester, "I am a poor brother of the Order of Saint Francis who comes here to do my duty to certain unhappy prisoners now held within this castle."

Front-de-Boeuf, whose family controlled this castle, had a servant bring the priest upstairs to where Cedric and Athelstane were locked up. "Why not let them see a priest? They'll soon be dead!" he told his comrades.

The moment Wamba was left alone with his master and his master's friend, he revealed himself and the next step of the plan. "Take this hooded cloak, good Cedric, and march quietly out of the castle, leaving me *your* cloak and belt."

"Leave you in my place!" said Cedric, astonished. "Why, they would hang you, poor knave.—But don't save me; save the noble Athelstane, my trusty Wamba! It is the duty of each who has Saxon blood in his veins to save him. He would be king had the Normans stayed in France where they belonged. You and I will remain imprisoned, while he, free and safe, shall round up our countrymen to either save us or avenge us."

"I came to save *you,* my master," said the jester, "but if you will not let me do that, I'll leave and save my own skin. You cannot pass my gift to you to him. I'll hang for no man but my own born master."

"Go, then, noble Cedric," said Athelstane, "do not give up this chance. You may be able to direct our friends how to rescue us."

"And is there any chance, then, of rescue?" said Cedric, looking at the jester.

"A half a chance, perhaps!" cried Wamba. "And so farewell. Remember, Cedric, that I flung away my life for my master, like a faithful . . . fool."

The exchange of clothes was now made, and Cedric started off on his quest to get out of the castle. He was stopped on his way, however, by Front-de-Boeuf's wife, Ulrica. She was the daughter of Torquil Wolfganger, a Saxon much respected by Cedric; Torquil had been murdered long ago by Front-de-Boeuf. Gray-haired Ulrica recognized old Cedric, even under the heavy brown hood, and promised her father's friend to help him in his battle against the Normans and against her husband. She claimed she had been unwillingly married to Front-de-Boeuf and kept captive within that very castle for dozens of years. But she meant now, she said, to have her revenge.

"There is a force outside," she told Cedric, "ready to attack this castle. Hurry and lead them to the battle, and when you see a red flag wave from the turret on the eastern angle of the main tower, attack with all your might— the Normans will then be busy trying to deal with the chaos I have created inside, and you may break through and defeat them."

Five minutes after Cedric had passed through the castle gates, De Bracy, wondering if that old hermit had tricked him, rushed to the room where Athelstane and Wamba were locked in.

"And what has happened to Cedric, you knave!" he screamed at Wamba.

"Am I not Cedric?" said Wamba.

De Bracy roared a curse on all jesters, and then hurried out, calling to his men and comrades that the preparations for battle were to proceed at double-time. "The outlaws have Cedric with them—he has escaped through the trickery of that would-be priest!" The Norman soldiers and knights hurried to guard the castle from immediate attack.

Meanwhile, above in the locked tower containing Rebecca and Ivanhoe, the disinherited son came to his senses, revived by tender nursing and fitting medicines. Ivanhoe could hear the heavy steps of men in armor and the voices of knights and their shouts. He yearned to join the battle against the heartless Normans and to save his father and Rowena.

"If I could but drag myself," he said to Rebecca, "to yonder window, I might see how this battle proceeds! But I am helpless here."

"Do not fret, noble knight," answered Rebecca, "the sounds have suddenly stopped."

"This dead pause only shows that the men are at their posts on the walls, and expecting instant attack," replied Ivanhoe. "Could I but reach yonder window!"

"You would injure yourself if you tried," said his nurse. "I will stand at the window and describe to you what passes outside."

"You must not—you shall not!" exclaimed Ivanhoe. "Each window will be soon a mark for the archers; you could be—"

Rebecca ignored him and climbed the three steps which led to the window.

"Rebecca, dear Rebecca!" pleaded Ivanhoe, "this is no

maiden's pastime—do not expose yourself to wounds and death; at least cover yourself with yonder ancient shield, and show as little of yourself as may be."

Following the directions of Ivanhoe, Rebecca used the shield against the lower part of the window, and reported to him the preparations which their friends, the attackers, were making. "The edge of the forest seems lined with archers, although only a few are advanced from its dark shadows. I see a knight in black armor at the front. He seems to be the leader.—God of Zion protect us!—What a dreadful sight!—Those who advance first bear huge shields; the others follow, bending their bows as they come on.—They raise their bows!"

Her description was here suddenly interrupted by the signal for attack, which was given by the blast of a shrill bugle, and at once answered by a blaring flourish of the Norman trumpets from the castle battlements. Both sides shouted war-cries. The followers of Front-de-Boeuf defended the castle from the furious attack, and answered the arrows from Locksley's men with shots from their cross-bows and slings.

"What do you see, Rebecca?" demanded the wounded knight.

"Nothing but the cloud of arrows flying so thick as to dazzle my eyes, and to hide the bowmen who shoot them.—Oh, now I see the Black Knight leading a group of men in pulling down the outer barrier across the moat. They have made a breach in the wall—they rush in—they are thrust back!—Front-de-Boeuf heads the defenders; I see his gigantic form. It is the meeting of two fierce tides—the conflict of two oceans moved by contrary winds! Holy prophets! Front-de-Boeuf and the Black Knight fight hand to hand in the opening of the wall, amid the roar of their followers." She then uttered a shriek, and exclaimed, "He is down!—he is down!"

"*Who* is down?" cried Ivanhoe.

"The Black Knight," answered Rebecca. "But no—but no!—the name of the Lord be blessed!—he is on foot

Peeking out from the window, Rebecca exclaimed:
"His sword is broken—he snatches an axe from a soldier——"

again, and fights as if there were twenty men's strength in his single arm.—His sword is broken—he snatches an axe from a soldier—he attacks Front-de-Boeuf with blow after blow.—The giant stoops and totters like an oak under the blade of the woodman—he falls—he falls!"

"Front-de-Boeuf?"

"Front-de-Boeuf!" answered Rebecca. "His men rush to the rescue, headed by Bois-Guilbert—they attack in return and force the Black Knight to back off—they drag Front-de-Boeuf within the walls."

"The attackers have crossed the outer walls, have they not?"

"They have!" exclaimed Rebecca. "And they press on; some plant ladders, some try to climb upon the shoulders of each other—but down go stones, beams, and trunks of trees upon their heads! The Black Knight approaches the outer door with his huge axe. The thundering blows which he deals, can you hear them above all the din and shouts of the battle?—Stones and beams are thrown down on the bold champion—he regards them no more than if they were feathers! The outer gate shakes—it crashes—it is splintered by his blows—they rush in—the outer ground is won by the attackers."

"The bridge across the moat into the castle—have they captured that?"

"No," replied Rebecca. "Bois-Guilbert has destroyed the plank on which they crossed.—The battle is over for a time. Our friends strengthen themselves within the outwork which they have won. It affords them a good shelter from the castle defenders."

Ivanhoe's hunger for battle and his deep wounds which prevented any action from him soon wore him out, and before the battle resumed, he fell asleep.

Rebecca wrapped herself in her veil, and sat down at a distance from the couch of the wounded knight.

4. "The Castle Burns!"

A S SOON AS Cedric reached the Black Knight and Locksley they greeted him, congratulating him on his escape. He told them of Ulrica's promise to help them. They were glad to know they had a friend within the castle.

Locksley, the great bowman, had the leadership of the archers, while the Black Knight led the rest. Cedric, though a brave warrior, knew little of the strategy of battle and agreed to follow the Black Knight, who ordered the building of a long raft. The knight hoped to be able to cross the moat on the raft in spite of the fierce resistance of the enemy. The raft-building took quite some time, but when it was ready, the Black Knight spoke to his followers: "It does no good to wait here any longer, my friends—the sun is moving towards the west and will soon be setting. I have many duties I must attend to, and so I must go away by tomorrow. One of you go to Locksley, and ask him to begin firing arrows on the opposite side of the castle and move forward as if about to rush into it; and you, true English hearts, stand by me, and be ready to thrust the raft into the moat. Follow me boldly across, and help me burst that lower door in the main wall of the castle."

In another moment, the knight ordered the outer gate opened, and they launched the raft, a sort of floating bridge from the land across the moat.

Well aware of the importance of taking the foe by surprise, the Black Knight, closely followed by Cedric, threw

37

The two warriors hacked away at the main wall,
dodging arrows showered at the castle.

himself onto the raft and reached the opposite side. Here
he began to thunder with his axe upon the gate of the castle. The followers of the Black Knight and Cedric had less
luck in crossing and had to turn back. The two warriors
were alone hacking away at the main wall for a time, but
to distract the soldiers high above from attacking their
vulnerable leaders, the Saxon rebels showered arrows
upon the castle windows and heights.

"Shame on you all!" cried De Bracy, who was Prince
John's Norman adviser. He shouted at his soldiers upon

the castle walls: "Do you call yourselves bowmen, and let these two dogs keep their place at our very door?"

At this moment the attackers caught sight of the red flag upon the angle of the tower which Ulrica had described to Cedric.

"To the charge, bold comrades!" cried Locksley. "The castle is ours, we have friends within. See yonder flag, it is the signal—Torquilstone Castle is ours!"

With that he bent his bow and sent a shaft through the breast of one of the soldiers who, under De Bracy's direction, were loosening a fragment from one of the battlements to drop on the heads of Cedric and the Black Knight. The other soldiers became careful not to put themselves in plain sight of Locksley, as their armor seemed no use against the shot of this tremendous archer.

"Do not give ground, you knaves!" said De Bracy. He himself snatched up the lever to loosen the piece of battlement. All below saw the danger, and the boldest, even Friar Tuck, avoided setting foot on the raft to go across the moat. Three times did Locksley shoot at De Bracy, and three times did the arrow bound back from the knight's armor.

"I curse your Spanish steel-coat!" said Locksley. He then began to call, "Comrades! Noble Cedric! Black Knight! Watch out for the falling stones!"

Locksley's warning would have come too late; the massive stonework already tottered, and De Bracy, who still heaved at prying it loose, would have finally succeeded had not he heard the voice of Brian de Bois-Guilbert.

"All is lost, De Bracy. The castle burns."

"What is to be done!" shouted De Bracy.

"Listen to me. Lead your men down, as if to fight; throw the castle gate open—there are only two men on the raft, and fling them into the moat, and push across to the land. I will charge from the main gate and attack on the outside."

De Bracy hastily drew his men together, and rushed down to the massive door, which he caused instantly to be thrown open. But the moment this was done the Black Knight forced his way inward.

"Dogs!" said De Bracy to his men, "will you let two men prevent us from reaching our only way to safety?"

"But he is the devil himself!" said a soldier.

"And if he is the devil," replied De Bracy, "would you fly from him into the mouth of flames? The castle burns behind us—let despair give you courage, or let me forward, and I will cope with this champion myself."

De Bracy jumped forward and he was now fighting hand to hand with the Black Knight. De Bracy with his sword and the Black Knight with his axe were giving each other furious blows. At length the Norman received a blow which, though its force was partly blocked by his shield, fell yet with such force on his helmet that he tumbled to the paved floor.

"Give up, De Bracy," said the Black Champion, stooping over him, and holding against the bars of his helmet the fatal dagger with which knights killed their enemies. "Give up, Maurice De Bracy, or you are a dead man."

"I will not give up to a nameless man," replied De Bracy. "Tell me who you are, or do as you like."

The Black Knight whispered something into his ear. "I give up," answered the Norman.

"Go to the gate, and there wait my further orders," said the mysterious Black Knight.

"Before I do, let me tell you," said De Bracy, "that Wilfred of Ivanhoe is wounded, and a prisoner, and will perish in the burning castle without immediate help."

"Wilfred of Ivanhoe!" exclaimed the Black Knight. "The life of every man in the castle shall answer for it if a hair on his head is singed. Where is his chamber?"

"Ascend yonder winding stair," said De Bracy. "It leads to his room."

During this combat, and the brief conversation between

the leaders, Cedric, at the head of a body of men, had pushed across the bridge, driving back the dispirited followers of De Bracy.

As the fire grew, smoke began to seep into the room where Ivanhoe was tended by Rebecca. He had been awakened from his slumber by the noise of the battle, and his nurse, who had again placed herself at the window to watch and report to him the fate of the attack, was for some time prevented from observing either by the billows of smoke.

"The castle burns!" said Rebecca. "What can we do to save ourselves?"

"Flee, Rebecca, and save your own life," said Ivanhoe, "for no help can save me."

"I will not flee," she answered. "We will be saved or perish together.—And yet, great God!—my father—my father! What will happen to him?"

At this moment the door of the room flew open, and Bois-Guilbert presented himself—a ghastly figure, for his gilded armor was dented, pierced and bloody, and the feather atop his helmet was partly cut away, partly burnt. "I have found you," he said to Rebecca. "There is but one path to safety; I have cut my way through fifty dangers to bring you through it—now follow me."

"Alone," answered Rebecca, "I will not follow you. Save also my father and this wounded knight."

The Templar laughed at her, and seized her, in spite of her shrieks, and in spite of the worthless threats Ivanhoe thundered against him. "You dog of the Temple!—Set free the damsel!—Traitor!—It is Ivanhoe who commands you!"

A moment or two after the Templar's escape, the Black Knight appeared in the doorway. "I would not have found you, Wilfred," said the Black Knight, "but for your shouts."

"Think not of me, my lord," said Wilfred, "pursue that villain—but first rescue Cedric and Rowena."

"In their turn," answered the Black Knight; "but yours is first."

And seizing upon Ivanhoe, he bore him off with as much ease as the Templar had carried off Rebecca, rushed with him down the stairs to the gates, and having there delivered the young man to the care of two rebels, he again entered the smoking castle to help in the rescue of the other prisoners.

One turret was now in bright flames, which flashed out furiously from window and shot-hole. Through the scene

Rebecca rode with Bois-Guilbert, his left arm clasped against her, his right arm wielding a vicious sword.

of confusion, Cedric rushed in quest of Rowena, while the faithful swineherd Gurth, following him closely, ignored his own safety while he blocked the blows that were aimed at his master. The noble Saxon was able to reach his ward's apartment just as she had given up all hopes of safety. He now asked Gurth to lead her to the outer gate, the passage to which was now free of enemies and not yet too fiery to cross. This done, Cedric hurried to find his friend Athelstane. But before Cedric reached as far as the old hall in which he had himself been a prisoner, Wamba the jester had freed himself and Athelstane.

In the meantime, Bois-Guilbert had leapt onto his horse in the courtyard. "Come along!" he shouted to his own men, who either quickly mounted on their horses, or ran alongside. Rebecca, nearly in a faint, rode with Bois-Guilbert, his left arm clasped against her, his right arm wielding a vicious sword. Though a kidnapper and bloody-minded warrior, he showed every concern for her safety, and little for his own.

He spurred the horse forward, struck down the first of the Saxon attackers, and rushed on, leading his men through and past the various arrows and sword thrusts.

Athelstane, freed from his captivity, was eager to contribute to the Saxon fight against the Normans, and when he saw the woman in Bois-Guilbert's saddle, he was sure it must be Rowena.

"I will rescue her from yonder cruel knight, and he shall die by my hand!" he declared. Athelstane snatched a mace that had fallen to the ground, and rushed at Bois-Guilbert. "Terrible Templar! Let her go!"

"You Saxon dog!" said Bois-Guilbert. Stopping and turning his snorting steed, he rose in his stirrups and then gave a powerful blow of his sword to Athelstane's head. The Saxon fell to the ground.

Bois-Guilbert called out, "Whoever wants to escape these Saxon fiends, follow me!" He pushed across the drawbridge, swinging his sword with such strength and deadliness that the archers blocking his path leapt out of his way. He was followed by a dozen armored soldiers, who upon their horses galloped off with him.

The fire was spreading rapidly throughout the castle when Ulrica, the bold woman who had started it, appeared on a turret croaking out a Saxon war-song. Her long gray hair streamed out behind her in the breeze. The towering flames seemed to reach the evening skies. When tower after tower began to crash down, the fighters were driven from the courtyard by the heavy debris. The defeated Normans, of whom very few remained alive, scattered and escaped into the neighboring forest. All the prisoners but Athelstane had been saved from death. Friar Tuck pulled poor broken-hearted Isaac from the dungeon not long after the Templar had escaped with Isaac's daughter. The victors gazed with wonder upon the fiery castle.

"The den of tyrants is no more!" cried Locksley. "Let each of you fine fighters bring his loot to the Trysting Tree. In the morning we will divvy up our shares."

Before the sun had risen the next morning, the Black Knight had brought Ivanhoe to a priory, where the kindly priests would try to nurse him back to health. Locksley's brave outlaws, in the meanwhile, were gathering around the Trysting Tree. There had been much loot to gather from the large castle, even though much more of it had been burned.

Locksley took his place on a seat of grass under the twisted branches of the huge oak tree, and gave the seats of honor on his right and left to the Black Knight and Cedric the Saxon.

"In the forest, my noble friends," he said, "I am the king. I hope that does not offend you."

The Black Knight laughed and said, "Not at all!"

Cedric agreed.

"Then, Cedric," continued Locksley, "observe that our collected booty is divided into two portions. Choose that which you prefer, to repay your men who helped us overcome the Normans in this adventure."

"Good man," said Cedric, "my heart is filled with sadness. The noble Athelstane, would-be king of the Saxons, is no more, killed in yesterday's action. My people are only awaiting to bring his honored remains to Rotherwood. I have stayed until now only to thank you."

The tramp of horsemen was now heard, and Lady Rowena appeared, surrounded by several riders. "God bless you, brave men," she told Locksley and his followers. "We thank you for helping the oppressed of England. If any of you forest-dwellers should hunger, remember I have food to offer—and if the Normans drive you from these glades, I have forests of my own where you, my gallant rescuers, may wander and hunt as you like."

"Thanks, gentle lady," said Locksley. "But to have saved you is pay enough in itself."

Bowing from her horse, Rowena turned to depart, while Cedric also said goodbye, telling the Black Knight, "I know that you wandering knights do not like to stop over anywhere long, but a home is sometimes desirable. You have earned hospitality for as long as you will in my mansion at Rotherwood, noble knight."

"To Rotherwood I will come, brave Saxon, and soon; but pressing matters prevent me from riding along with you now," replied the Black Knight. "When I do come, I will ask a favor."

"It is granted before it is asked," said Cedric. "I have to say that during the funeral rites of Athelstane, I shall be living at his castle of Coningsburgh. Those halls will be open to you as well." A few moments later, Cedric and Rowena and their servants were moving off through the forest.

"Valiant warrior," Locksley addressed the Black Knight, "without your good heart and mighty arm, we would have lost the fight. Will you take something from that mass of loot?"

The Black Knight refused to choose from among the riches.

"Nothing? You must be richer than I thought!" laughed Locksley. "But I will give you a gift." The chief outlaw now took from his own neck a horn, and said, "Noble friend, please accept this bugle. If you have any need or trouble within this forest, blow three notes upon the horn like so, *Wa-sa-hoa!* and my men shall help you."

"Thank you for your gift," said the knight, "and better help than yours and your rangers would I never seek." And then he blew the horn till all the greenwood rang.

"Comrades," announced Locksley, "remember those notes—it is the call of the Black Knight."

"Long live the Black Knight!" shouted the outlaws.

The Black Knight got on his horse and waved, bidding his friends goodbye.

5. The Trial of Rebecca

MEANWHILE, Isaac of York, mounted upon a mule, the gift of the outlaw Locksley, with two men to act as his guard and guides, set out for Templestowe, the court housing the Knights of the Temple. He had learned that the wicked Bois-Guilbert had brought Rebecca there. He hoped that he would either be able to persuade the Templar or offer enough in ransom to free her.

The knights' castle-fortress lay in the midst of pretty meadows. Two soldiers, dressed in black, guarded the drawbridge, and many others paced back and forth upon the wall. When Isaac arrived at this forbidding place, he paused at the gate, well aware that the Templars, though supposedly good Christians, made it their sport to persecute Jews.

Within the walls of Templestowe at this time was visiting the Grand Master of all Templars. He had a long gray beard, with shaggy gray eyebrows. Though elderly, he was still fierce and pitiless. It was to him, the grim Grand Master, that Isaac, having bribed his way into the castle, was presented.

"What is your business, fellow?" asked the Grand Master.

"I pray for the return of my daughter."

"Your daughter! Here!?"

"One of your own Templars, Brian de Bois-Guilbert, has kidnapped her."

47

The Grand Master was furious. Until this moment he had known nothing of Bois-Guilbert's action. But he was less angry with the knight than he was with this old man and the unlucky woman! He thought and thought, before replying, "She must be a witch to have bewitched one of the Temple's finest soldiers into falling in love with her."

"No, gracious sir! She is no witch. She is, in fact, a healer—a physician."

"Even worse! A double-witch!"

"No, she was taught the art of medicine by Miriam, a wise old woman of our tribe."

"Silence!" said the Grand Master. "Just as Miriam—I remember her!—was burnt at the stake, so shall your daughter! I will teach her to throw spells over the soldiers of the blessed Temple. We will judge and condemn her as a witch." He ordered his men to throw Isaac out of the building.

"The witch," announced the Grand Master to his followers, "shall be killed, and the wickedness she brought here shall be forgiven. Prepare the Castle-hall for the trial of the sorceress."

Within hours the Temple's workmen had built in the great hall a platform for the judges to sit upon and benches for the knights. The trial of the innocent and unhappy Rebecca shortly followed. On an elevated chair, directly before the accused, sat the Grand Master, in white robes, holding in his hand a staff. At his feet was placed a table, occupied by two scribes, whose duty it was to record the proceedings. The four preceptors, or teaching masters of the Temple, sat at either side of the Grand Master. The Temple knights were on benches below, while onlookers filled the rest of the hall, each to watch the unusual scene of a Grand Master and Jewish sorceress encounter each other. There was a deep choral chant before the proceedings began.

"Unhappy man!" said the Grand Master to an attendant as he glanced at Brian de Bois-Guilbert. "You see how he cannot look upon us; he cannot look upon her. He is bewitched."

The Grand Master then raised his voice and addressed the assembly: "Good and valiant men, knights, preceptors, and friends of this Holy Order! Be it known to you, that with this baton I hold, we have full power to judge and to try all that regards the well-being of our Holy Order. When the wolf has attacked a member of the flock, it is the duty of the kind shepherd to call his comrades together, that with bows and arrows they may stop the invader. We have therefore summoned to our presence a Jewish woman, by name Rebecca, daughter of Isaac of York—a woman infamous for witchery; using such, she has stirred the heart and confused the brain of one of our most esteemed knights. If we had been told that a man as honored by us as Brian de Bois-Guilbert suddenly cast away regard for his character, his vows, his brothers of the Temple, his prospects by chasing after a Jewish damsel, by defending her safety in preference to his own and finally was so utterly blinded by his madness to hide her in our own Temple, what should we say but that the noble knight was possessed by some evil demon or charmed by some wicked spell? Were he not bewitched we would cut him off and cast him from our brotherhood.—However, we blame her spells and feel sorry for his fall. We now call witnesses of these unhappy doings, that we may judge whether we may punish this woman."

Several witnesses were called upon to describe the risks to which Bois-Guilbert put himself in saving Rebecca from the blazing castle. The head preceptor of the Temple was then called on to describe the manner in which Bois-Guilbert and the Jewess arrived at Templestowe. He suggested that Bois-Guilbert had lately seemed crazed.

Another preceptor declared, "I would like to know, Grand Master, what Brian de Bois-Guilbert says to these accusations, and how he sees himself in regard to the Jewish maiden."

The Grand Master commanded the Templar to answer, but Bois-Guilbert remained silent.

"He is possessed by a devil preventing his speech!" declared the Grand Master. "Out, Satan!—Speak, Brian de Bois-Guilbert, I tell you, by this symbol of our Holy Order."

"I refuse to answer such wild charges," said the knight.

"Since our brother of the Temple has avoided our questions, let us continue on our quest to reach the bottom of this mystery," said the Grand Master. "Let those who have anything to say of the life and conversation of this Jewish woman stand forth before us."

A poor peasant, Saxon by birth, was dragged forward on his crutches from the crowd. He was forced to admit

A poor peasant, Saxon by birth,
was dragged forward on his crutches from the crowd.

that two years since, when residing at York, he was suddenly afflicted with a disease. He had been unable to stir from his bed until Rebecca had treated him and given him an ointment that had helped him move his arms and legs again. "May it please your graciousness," the old man concluded, "I cannot think the damsel meant harm by me."

"Silence, peasant!" said the Grand Master, "and begone! I tell you, the witch can bring on diseases for the very purpose of removing them!"

Other witnesses came and followed, but none of them had anything remarkable to say about Rebecca's powers, in spite of the Grand Master's peculiar way of twisting their statements. Finally, he commanded Rebecca to unveil herself.

Opening her lips for the first time, she replied, "It is not the custom of the daughters of my people to uncover our faces in the assembly of strangers." The sweet tones of her voice and the softness of her reply made the audience sympathize with and pity her. The Grand Master, however, ignored his own better feelings and commanded again that his victim be unveiled. The guards were about to remove her veil when she stood up and said, "No, let me not be thus handled! I will obey you myself and show you the features of an ill-fated maiden."

She withdrew her veil and looked on them with shyness and dignity. Her beauty excited a murmur of surprise. Several knights said to each other, "It's no wonder to me now why Bois-Guilbert has risked his career for her!" Further witnesses were brought on. They testified to having heard her mutter to herself in an unknown language—that the songs she sung were of a strangely sweet sound, which made the ears of the hearer tingle and his heart throb— that she spoke at times to herself, and seemed to look upward for reply—that her clothes were strange—that she wore rings and odd embroidery on her veils.

All these details, so natural and so normal for a woman of her background, were gravely listened to by the judges as proofs that Rebecca was a witch.

The Grand Master now in a solemn tone demanded of Rebecca what she had to say against the sentence he was about to pronounce.

"To ask for your pity," said the lovely woman, with a trembling voice, "would, I am aware, be useless. To state that to relieve the sick and wounded cannot be displeasing to the Founder of our faiths would not help either. It would do no good to explain that the peculiarities of my dress, language, and manners are those of my people. Nor will I even declare my innocence in contrast to my kidnapper, Brian de Bois-Guilbert, who stands there listening to the words which seem to convert his victim into the guilty one. God will be judge between him and me! I will not therefore turn the charge against him but ask him himself whether the accusations brought against me are not false?"

There was a pause. All eyes turned to him. He was silent.

"Speak!" she said, "if you are a man—if you are a Christian, speak! Tell if these things are true!"

"Answer her, brother," said the Grand Master.

But he did not speak.

"Rebecca," said the Grand Master, "you can gain nothing from a statement by an unhappy knight, for whom, as we well perceive, your charms are too powerful. Have you anything else to say?"

"There is yet one chance left to me," said Rebecca, "even by your own fierce laws. I deny this charge. I maintain my innocence, and I declare the falsehood of this accusation. I know that I may choose combat rather than this trial to determine my fate. Someone will fight to prove my innocence."

"And who, Rebecca," replied the Grand Master, "will use his lance for a sorceress? Who will be the defender of a Jewess?"

"God will raise me up a champion," said Rebecca. "It cannot be that in England there will not be found one to fight for justice. I declare my choice of combat over this trial."

With those words, she took her embroidered glove from her hand and flung it down before the Grand Master.

He nearly jumped out of his chair. "Damsel," he said, "repent! Admit your wrongdoing! Confess your witch-

"Damsel," the Grand Master said,
"repent! Admit your wrongdoing and confess your witchcraft!"

craft—turn from your evil faith—embrace Christianity, and all shall be well. In some convent you shall have time for prayer and penance. What has your religion done for you that you should die for it?"

"It was the religion of my fathers," said Rebecca; "it was delivered in thunders and in storms upon the mountain of

Sinai, in cloud and in fire. I am a maiden, unskilled to dispute for my religion, but I can die for it, if it be God's will.—Let me have an answer to my demand of a champion."

"Brothers," the Grand Master spoke, "you are aware that we might well refuse this woman the benefit of a trial by combat, but since we are knights and soldiers as well as men of religion, it would be a shame to refuse. This, therefore, is the case. Rebecca, daughter of Isaac of York, is accused of sorcery practiced upon a noble knight of our Holy Order, and has offered combat to prove her innocence. Whom, brothers, should we name to be our champion on the field?"

"Brian de Bois-Guilbert, whom it chiefly concerns," said a preceptor. "He best knows how the truth stands in this matter. No spell of hers can affect the champion who comes forward to fight for the judgment of God."

"You say what is right, brother," said the Grand Master. "It is our requirement of you, brother," he continued, addressing Bois-Guilbert, "that you do your battle as well as you are able. We all know that the good cause shall triumph.—And you, Rebecca, be advised that you have three days from today to find a champion. The battle must be fought before us, and weighty causes call us away on the fourth day."

"God's will be done," said Rebecca. "I will put my trust in Him."

She was allowed to write a letter to her father before she was taken away captive till that fateful day.

6. Athelstane's Ghost

WHEN THE Black Knight left the Trysting Tree of Locksley, he made his way to the priory of Saint Botolph, where he had taken the wounded Ivanhoe when the castle was captured and destroyed.

"We will meet again," the Black Knight told Ivanhoe, "at Coningsburgh, the castle of Athelstane, since your father holds the funeral feast for his noble relation there. It shall be my task to reconcile you and your father."

"Please let me go along with you now," said Ivanhoe, his voice weak.

The Black Knight would not listen to this proposal. "Rest today, Ivanhoe. You will have hardly enough strength enough to travel tomorrow. I will have no guide but Wamba, who can play priest or fool, whichever I am most in the mood for."

Later that morning, Ivanhoe requested to see the prior. The old man came in haste, and asked after the knight's health.

"It is better," said Ivanhoe, "than my fondest hope; either my wound has been slighter than the bleeding led me to suppose, or this soothing ointment of Rebecca's has amazingly cured it. I feel already as if I could put on my armor."

"We cannot let the son of Cedric leave our convent before his wounds are healed!" said the prior.

"I would not desire to leave, Prior, did I not feel able to

55

endure the journey. I mean to accompany the Black Knight, whom I fear will face some terrible challenge."

And so he left that morning on the prior's mule, accompanied by the swineherd Gurth, who carried the knight's armor.

Meanwhile, Wamba and the Black Knight were deep into the forest when the jester noticed some men in hiding. "I have two or three times noticed the glance of a helmet among the green leaves," said Wamba. "If they were honest men, they would be on the path."

"I believe you are right," said the knight, closing his visor.

And it is good he did close it, for three arrows flew at the same instant from the suspected spot against his head

Wamba and the Black Knight were deep into the forest when the jester noticed some men in hiding.

and breast, one of which would have pierced his brain had it not been turned aside by the steel visor. The other two bounced off the helmet's collar.

The knight said to Wamba, "To the fight!" and rode straight at the hiding place. He was met by six or seven horsemen in armor, who ran against him with their lances. Three of the weapons struck against him and splintered as if they had been driven against a tower of steel. The Black Knight's eyes seemed to flash fire through the window of his visor. He raised himself in his stirrups and exclaimed, "What do you mean by this attack?"

"Die, tyrant!" they cried.

"Ha!" said the Black Knight, striking down man after man. "Are you traitors?"

Suddenly one of the knights, in blue armor, spurred forward with his lance and took aim not at the rider but at the steed, wounding the noble animal.

"That was a cowardly strike!" exclaimed the Black Knight.

At this same moment, Wamba blew the Black Knight's bugle, the gift of Locksley, which he had been carrying for his new master. The attacking knights resumed their fight with the Black Knight and the jester, who were pressed very closely by so many men at the same time. Then an arrow suddenly stretched on the earth one of the strongest of the attackers, and a band of merry men broke forth from the glade, headed by Locksley and Friar Tuck, who soon knocked down the ruffians, all of whom lay on the spot dead or wounded.

The Black Knight thanked his rescuers, and said, "I need to discover who these unprovoked enemies were.— Open the visor of that Blue Knight, Wamba. He seems to be the chief of these villains."

With no gentle hand, Wamba undid the helmet of the Blue Knight, revealing a face the Black Knight did not expect to see.

"Waldemar Fitzurse!" he said to his former friend. "What could bring you to so wicked an action?"

"Richard," said the captive, "you know little of mankind if you do not know to what crimes ambition and revenge can lead."

"Revenge?" said the Black Knight. "I never wronged you.—Who set you on this traitorous deed?"

"Your brother," answered Waldemar.

"I will not kill you, but you must leave within three days from England to your Norman castle, and never again mention John as connected with your crime. If you are found on English ground after the time I have given you, you die on the spot.—Let this knight have a steed, Locksley, for I see your men have caught those which were running loose, and let him depart unharmed."

"I would rather send an arrow after that villain and spare him the labor of a long journey," answered Locksley.

"You are bound to obey me," replied the Black Knight, "for I now announce to you that I am Richard the Lion-Hearted, King of England."

At these words, the merry men kneeled down before him and asked pardon for their offences.

"Rise, my friends," said Richard. "Your little trespasses have been forgiven by the loyal services you gave my distressed subjects at Torquilstone. Arise, my men, and be good subjects in the future.—And you, brave Locksley——"

"Call me no longer Locksley, my King, but know me by the name which fame has given me—I am Robin Hood, of Sherwood Forest."

"King of Outlaws!" said Richard. "Who has not heard this name which has been carried as far as Palestine? But be assured, brave outlaw, that no deed done in my long absence shall be held against you."

At this time, two more people appeared, Ivanhoe, on the prior's mule, and Gurth, who served him, on the knight's own warhorse. The astonishment of Ivanhoe was beyond bounds when he saw his master besprinkled with blood and six or seven dead bodies lying around in the little glade in which the battle had taken place.

*The merry men kneeled down before the Black Knight
and asked pardon for their offences.*

"Come forward, Wilfred," said Richard, "and meet these
true English hearts."

"Sir Wilfred of Ivanhoe," said Robin Hood, "let me say
that Richard has not truer subjects than those who now
stand around him."

"I cannot doubt it, brave man," said Ivanhoe, "since you
are here.—But what do these slain men mean, and the
bloody armor of my King?"

"Treason has been with us, Ivanhoe," said the King.
"But thanks to these brave men, treason has met its re-
ward. But now," he smiled, "I think you too are a traitor!
For were not my orders that you should stay at Saint
Botolph's until your wound was healed?"

"It *is* healed," said Ivanhoe. "It is now no more than a
scratch. But why, oh why, noble King, will you expose
your life to danger by lonely journeys and rash adven-
tures? Your kingdom would be threatened with civil war if
England lost you."

"Ho! ho!" answered Richard. "My best subjects disobey me and then lecture me!—Yet forgive my laughter, my faithful Wilfred. The time I have spent, and am yet to spend in hiding, is, as I explained to you, necessary to give my friends and faithful nobles time to assemble their forces, that when my return is announced, I should be at the head of such a force as enemies shall tremble to face, and thus put down the treason of my brother without even drawing a sword."

Ivanhoe bowed, and Richard addressed Robin Hood, "King of Outlaws, have you no food and drink to offer your brother king?"

Beneath a huge oak tree a meal was hastily prepared for the King of England, surrounded by outlaws to the government who now formed his court and his guard. Songs and jests were exchanged, and stories told. The merry King laughed, drank, and joked among the jolly band.

Soon after, Richard called for his helmet, gave his hand to Robin Hood and rode away with Wilfred and their serving men. That same evening they arrived at the Castle of Coningsburgh. There was a tremendous feast being prepared in honor of the slain Athelstane.

King Richard was shown into the castle, shortly followed by Ivanhoe, who hid his face in his cloak, as it had been decided that he should not present himself to his father until the King should give him the signal.

A dozen of the most important representatives of the Saxon families were gathered around a large oaken table. Most of the men were old, for the younger race, to the great displeasure of the seniors, had, like Ivanhoe, broken down many of the barriers which separated for half a century the Normans from the Saxons.

Cedric seemed to act as the chief of this group. Upon the entrance of Richard (only known to him as the Black Knight), he arose gravely and gave him welcome. He also welcomed the disguised Ivanhoe, who nodded, lest his father recognize his voice.

After a toast, Cedric conducted Richard and Ivanhoe into a small chapel, where two smoky torches lit up a coffin, on each side of which knelt priests muttering prayers. From there, Cedric led them to another chapel, where they met Athelstane's mother, Edith. The guests bowed deeply to the mourning parent, and withdrew with their guide. A winding stairway led them to another chamber, where about twenty matrons and maidens were listening to Rowena leading a choir of four in a hymn for Athelstane's soul.

After this, Cedric conducted his guests to a small room for distinguished visitors. He was about to withdraw when the Black Knight took his hand, saying, "I crave to remind you, noble Cedric, that when we last parted, you promised to grant me a favor."

Richard and Ivanhoe were conducted into the chapel, where priests muttered prayers by Athelstane's coffin.

"It is granted before it is named, noble knight," said Cedric. "Yet at this sad moment——"

"Of that also," said the Black Knight, "I have thought—but my time is brief. As yet you have known me as the Black Knight. Know me now as Richard Plantagenet."

"Richard!" exclaimed Cedric, stepping backward.

"Yes, Cedric, I am Richard, King of England. My deepest wish is to see my people united with each other. I ask of you, as a man of your word, to rebestow your fatherly love on the good knight Wilfred of Ivanhoe."

"And this is Wilfred!" said Cedric, pointing to his son.

"My father! my father!" said Ivanhoe, uncovering his head and kneeling at Cedric's feet. "Grant me your forgiveness."

"You have it, my son," said Cedric, raising him up. "I know how to keep my word, Richard, even when it has been passed to a Norman. But let me see you use the dress and costume of your English ancestry, Ivanhoe—no short cloaks, no fancy hats, no feathers. He that would be the son of Cedric must show himself of English ancestry. You are about to speak," he added sternly, "and I guess the topic. Lady Rowena must complete two years' mourning for Athelstane, the man I intended her to marry, before you may wed her. The ghost of Athelstane would burst from his coffin if we dishonored his memory."

It seemed as if Cedric's words had raised a ghost; for a moment after he had uttered them the door flew open, and Athelstane, dressed in his burial clothes, stood before them.

Cedric started back, staring. Ivanhoe crossed himself, while Richard said, "Bless me!"

"In the name of God!" said Cedric, "speak!"

"I will," said the ghost, "when I have collected my breath, and when you give me time.—I am as much alive as he can be who has been shut up in a box for three days."

"Noble Athelstane!" said Richard, "I myself saw you

*As if Cedric's words had raised a ghost, Athelstane,
dressed in his burial clothes, stood before them.*

struck down by the fierce Templar towards the end of the battle at Torquilstone, and as I thought, and Wamba reported, your skull was split in two."

"You were mistaken, Sir Knight," said Athelstane, "and Wamba misspoke. The Templar's sword turned in his hand, so that the blade struck me flat-ways. Down I went, stunned, indeed, but unwounded. I never recovered my senses until I found myself in a coffin—an open one, by good luck—placed before the altar. I pray you, good sirs, to fetch me a cup of wine."

The guests, though still wide-mouthed with astonishment, pledged a toast to their revived host. His mother and all the other guests soon hurried to the room to see the man they needed no longer mourn.

After more telling of his lost days, Athelstane was introduced to the King, to whom he swore loyalty. The revived man also now explained to Cedric that he had no intention of marrying Rowena, who, he was sure, preferred the forgiven Ivanhoe. "Ever since I awoke from that blow to my head," he remarked, "I seem to have come to my senses."

Before the celebration of Athelstane's life could begin, Ivanhoe was called away by none other than Isaac, who had tracked him down to this castle. Ivanhoe, Gurth, Richard, and Wamba set out before Athelstane had hardly been alive again to the world an hour.

7. The Fatal Contest

OUR SCENE now returns to the Templestowe Castle, about the hour when the life or death of Rebecca was to be decided. A crowd was watching the gate of the castle, while still greater numbers had already surrounded the field nearby. This field belonged to the Templars and had been leveled with care for military and chivalrous sports.

A throne had been erected for the Grand Master at the east end, with special seats for the preceptors and knights. At the opposite end of the field was a pile of firewood, arranged around a stake for the victim. With the crowd waiting for the contest between Brian de Bois-Guilbert and Rebecca's champion, a heavy bell rang from a nearby church.

At length the drawbridge fell, the gates opened, and a knight bearing the flag of the Order of Templars trotted out on a steed from the castle, preceded by six trumpets, and followed by the preceptors, two and two, the Grand Master coming last, mounted on a stately horse. Behind that old, cold-hearted man came Bois-Guilbert, in bright armor, but without his lance, shield, and sword, which were carried along by two esquires behind him. His face, though partly hidden by a long plume which floated down from his cap, looked ghastly pale, as if he had not slept for several nights.

On either side rode his comrades, and behind them followed other knights of the Templars and servants. Finally came a guard of jailers on foot, in black robes, in the middle of whom was Rebecca. A coarse white simple dress had been substituted for her Eastern garments; yet there was such courage in her look that each person that gazed upon her wept.

Rebecca entered the field in the slow procession, ready for judgment.

This slow procession entered the field and marched once around, and when they had completed the circle, made a halt. There was then a momentary bustle, while the Grand Master and all his attendants, except Bois-Guilbert, got off their horses. Poor Rebecca was conducted to the black chair placed near the pile of firewood.

Meanwhile, the Grand Master had assumed his seat; and when the knights all around him were seated as well, a loud and long flourish of trumpets announced that the Court was ready for judgment. Malvoisin, one of the preceptors, stepped forward and laid Rebecca's glove, which was the pledge of battle, at the feet of the Grand Master.

"Reverend Father," said Malvoisin, "here stands Brian de Bois-Guilbert, Knight of the Order of the Temple, who, by accepting the pledge of battle which I now lay at your reverence's feet, has become bound to do his duty in combat today, to maintain that this Jewish maiden, by name Rebecca, has justly deserved the doom passed upon her by this most Holy Order of the Temple of Zion, condemning her to die as a witch."

"Has he made his oath that his quarrel is just and honorable?" asked the Grand Master.

"He has sworn to the truth of the accusation."

The Grand Master commanded the herald to do his duty.

"Hear ye, hear ye," called the herald. "The good knight, Brian de Bois-Guilbert, is ready to do battle with any knight who will take Rebecca's cause upon himself. To such a champion the Grand Master offers a fair field for fair combat."

A few moments passed in terrible silence.

"No champion appears for the accused," said the Grand Master. "Go, herald, and ask her whether she expects anyone to do battle for her in this cause."

"Damsel," said the herald, sympathizing with her in his heart, but speaking cold words, "are you prepared with a champion to do battle this day in your behalf, or do you yield as one justly condemned to doom?"

"I maintain my innocence," said Rebecca, "and do *not* yield myself as justly condemned."

"We will wait one hour to see if a champion shall appear for this unfortunate woman. When that time comes, let her prepare for death," declared the Grand Master.

Rebecca bowed her head, folded her arms and, looking up towards heaven, seemed to expect that aid from above which she could hardly expect from mankind.

During the awful wait that followed, Bois-Guilbert rode over and approached her, in spite of the scowls of his friends and the Grand Master. "Hear me, Rebecca," he whispered. "Mount behind me on my steed—and in one short hour, we will be away from all this. I will leave the Templars, and we together will flee England for the other side of Europe."

"Begone!" said Rebecca. "I hold you as my worst and most deadly enemy."

In surprise and disappointment, Bois-Guilbert backed his horse away and resumed his place.

It was the general belief that no one would or could appear for a Jewess accused of sorcery; and the knights began to whisper to each other that it was time to declare that the hour allotted for the trial by battle was over. At this instant, a knight, urging his horse to speed, appeared on the plain advancing toward the field. A hundred voices exclaimed, "A champion! a champion!"

The crowd shouted as the knight rode onto the field. Yet a second glance at him served to destroy the hope that his timely arrival had excited. His horse, urged for many miles to its utmost speed, appeared to stumble and sink from weariness, and the rider, slumping over as if in pain, seemed as weak as a lamb.

To the demand of the herald, who demanded his rank, his name and purpose, the stranger knight came forward and addressed the Grand Master and his preceptors in a voice that was almost breathless, "I am a knight who has come here to fight with lance and sword for this damsel, Rebecca, daughter of Isaac of York. I declare that the

The crowd shouted as the knight rode onto the field.

charges against her are false, and that Sir Brian de Bois-Guilbert is a traitor, murderer, and liar; and I will prove these statements on this field, with my body against his, by the aid of God."

"The stranger must first show," said the Grand Master, "that he comes from honorable parents. The Temple does not send forth her knights against nameless men."

"My name," said the knight, "is Wilfred of Ivanhoe."

"I will not fight with you at present," Bois-Guilbert called out. "Get your wounds healed, buy a sturdier horse, and it may be I will hold it worth my while to beat out of you this boyish foolishness."

"Ha! proud Templar," said Ivanhoe, "have you forgotten that twice you fell before this lance? Remember the fields at Acre—remember the passage of arms at Ashby? I will proclaim you a coward in every court in Europe—in every preceptory of your Order of the Templars, unless you do battle without further delay."

Bois-Guilbert exclaimed, looking fiercely at Ivanhoe, "Dog of a Saxon! Take your lance, and prepare for death!"

"Does the Grand Master allow me the combat?" said Ivanhoe.

"I may not deny what you have challenged," said the Grand Master, "provided the maiden accepts you as her champion."

"Rebecca," said Ivanhoe, riding up to her, "do you accept me for your champion?"

"I do," she said, "I do. I accept you as the champion whom Heaven has sent me. Yet, no—no—your wounds are not healed.—Do not try to fight that wicked man—why should you perish also?"

But Ivanhoe was already at his post, and had closed his visor and readied his lance. Bois-Guilbert did the same. The herald, then, seeing each champion in his place, uplifted his voice, repeating three times, "Do your duty, knights!" After the third cry he withdrew to one side of the field. The Grand Master, who held in his hand the symbol of combat, Rebecca's glove, now threw it onto the field and pronounced the fatal words, "Let the battle proceed."

The trumpets sounded, and the knights charged each other at full speed. The wearied horse of Ivanhoe, and its no less exhausted rider, went down, as all had expected, before the well-aimed lance and strong steed of the Templar. This outcome all had foreseen; but although the spear of Ivanhoe hardly glanced off the shield of Bois-Guilbert, that knight, to the astonishment of all who watched, reeled in his saddle, lost hold of his stirrups, and fell onto the field.

Ivanhoe, crawling out from under his fallen horse, was soon on his feet, hurrying to continue battle with his

*To the astonishment of all, Bois-Guilbert reeled in his saddle
and fell onto the field.*

sword. But his opponent did not get up. Wilfred, placing his right foot on his foe's chest, and the sword's point to his throat, commanded the Templar to surrender his cause, or die on the spot. Bois-Guilbert returned no answer.

*Wilfred placed his right foot on the Templar's chest,
commanding him to surrender.*

"Slay him not, Sir Knight," said the Grand Master. "We declare him vanquished."

The old man climbed down to the field, and commanded the attendants to take the helmet off Bois-Guilbert. His eyes were closed—he was dead!

"This is indeed a judgment of God!" said the Grand Master, his eyes glancing heavenward.

When the first moments of surprise were over, Wilfred of Ivanhoe demanded of the Grand Master, as judge of the field, if he had manfully and rightfully done his duty in the combat.

"Manfully and rightfully has it been done," said the Grand Master. "I pronounce the maiden free and guiltless."

From nearby there was suddenly a clattering of horses' feet, advancing in such number and so rapidly as to shake the ground before them. Lo and behold, King Richard, still disguised as the Black Knight, galloped onto the field. He was followed by numerous armored soldiers and knights.

"I am too late!" he said with disappointment. "I had meant to battle Bois-Guilbert myself.—Ivanhoe, was this right, to take on such a venture, and you almost unable to sit upon your saddle?"

"Heaven, my lord, not I," answered Ivanhoe, "has taken this proud man for its victim."

"Peace be with him," said Richard.

"Who is this Black Knight that dares interfere with my contest?" asked the Grand Master.

"The King of England!" said Richard.

All were astonished at these words.

The King continued, "Proud Master of the Templars, your hand is in the lion's mouth. Depart with your followers, or remain and behold our English justice."

The Knights of the Temple gathered around the Grand Master like sheep around a watch-dog when they hear the baying of the wolf. The King rode slowly along the line of Templar knights, calling aloud, "Among so many gallant knights, will none dare splinter a spear with Richard?"

The Grand Master announced, "The Brothers of the Temple do not fight with you, Richard of England. We depart now, harming no one." With these words, without awaiting a reply, the Grand Master turned away. Trumpets sounded and the knights moved off slowly to follow him.

During the confusion which came with the retreat of the Templars, Rebecca saw and heard nothing—she was locked in the arms of her father. She, whose fortunes had formed the principal interest of the day, now went off with Isaac unobserved, the attention of the crowd transferred to the Black Knight, who was now celebrated with "Long live Richard the Lion-Hearted, and down with the Templars!"

As for Prince John? He was sent away for a time to distant lands by the kindly, forgiving Richard. Soon after the King's return to the throne, he sent for Cedric the Saxon, who came to court and within seven days had given his consent to the marriage of his ward Rowena to his son, Wilfred of Ivanhoe.

The wedding of our hero, thus formally approved by his father, was celebrated in the noble Minster of York. The King himself attended as well as many high-born Normans and Saxons.

The second morning after the wedding, Rebecca came to call on Lady Rowena. "Lady of Ivanhoe," said Rebecca, "I am the unhappy Jewess for whom your husband risked his life against such fearful odds in the fields of Templestowe."

"Damsel," said Rowena, "Wilfred of Ivanhoe on that day paid back but in slight measure your healing charity towards him. Speak, is there anything else in which he or I can serve you?"

"Nothing," said Rebecca, "unless you will give him my grateful farewell."

"You are leaving England, then?" said Rowena.

"I leave it, lady, very soon. My father has a brother in Spain, and we will go there. This is no safe home for the children of my people."

"But you, maiden," said Rowena, "you who nursed the sick-bed of Ivanhoe surely can have nothing to fear in England."

"We must go," said Rebecca sadly. "Farewell."

"Oh, remain with us," said Rowena. "Allow the teaching of our Christian holy men to convert you from your religion, and I will then be nearly a sister to you."

The second morning after the wedding,
Rebecca came to call on Lady Rowena.

"No, my lady," answered Rebecca, "that may not be. I may not change the faith of my fathers like a garment unsuited to the climate in which I seek to dwell. I will devote my thoughts to Heaven, and my actions to works of kindness, tending the sick, feeding the hungry, and relieving the distressed. Tell this to your husband, should he ask after the fate of her whose life he saved."

She glided from the chamber, leaving Rowena surprised as if a vision had passed before her. The fair wife related the strange meeting to her husband, on whose mind it made a deep impression. Even so, he lived long and happily with Rowena, for they were attached to each other by the bonds of early affection, and they loved each other the more for the many obstacles which had kept them apart for so long.

Ivanhoe became an important knight in Richard's service, and the King granted him many honors. He might have been honored even more but for the premature death of the heroic Lion-Hearted, who fell in the battle of the Castle of Chaluz. The passing of generous Richard brought to an end as well all the good and useful projects which he had begun.